THE ADVENTURES OF

Sir Givret the Short

THE KNIGHTS' TALES

THE ADVENTURES OF

Sir Givret the Short

GERALD MORRIS

ILLUSTRATED BY

AARON RENIER

HOUGHTON MIFFLIN COMPANY
BOSTON 2008

Library of Congress Cataloging-in-Publication Data is on file.
ISBN-13: 978-0-618-77715-0

Manufactured in the United States of America
MP 10 9 8 7 6 5 4 3 2 1

FOR SONJA AND DIANE AND
GRANDMOTHER MORRIS, MY FAVORITE LIBRARIANS.

Contents

Chapter 1
That Little Fellow

In all England's history, the storytellers say, no king was ever as great as King Arthur. No castle was as splendid as Arthur's Camelot, and no king ever held such magnificent feasts and tournaments. Most of all, no king helped the poor and weak as Arthur did. All the knights of his court vowed to defend the defenseless. Among them were famous knights—like Sir Lancelot the Great,

Sir Kay the Loyal, and Sir Gawain the True—as well as others, like Sir Pellinore the Absentminded, Sir Griflet the Tidy, and Sir Caranos the Usually Washed. Whatever their special qualities, though, these knights brought justice to England and made King Arthur's reign the Golden Age of Adventures.

It was Easter when one adventure came to the court. King Arthur was holding a holiday feast at Camelot, when a herald—that's what they used to call messengers—appeared in the banquet hall. "O King Arthur Pendragon," the herald announced, "High King of All England, Protector of the Weak, Defender of the—"

"Yes, yes, here I am," interrupted the king. "May I help you?"

"I bring tidings of a most prodigious adventure: a hunt for a wonderly marvelous stag!" He could have said "I've come to tell you about an amazing

stag," but heralds always used difficult, flowery language. No one knows why.

"And what is so marvelous about this stag?" asked the king.

"Not only is the creature uncannily white in hue, but legend saith that the knight who captures this wondrous beast earns thereby the right to kiss the fairest damsel in the world!"

Arthur's knights looked puzzled. "You mean whoever catches this stag gets to kiss the most beautiful lady in the world?" asked the king.

"That's what I said," replied the herald. "But I prithee peradventure thou be aforewarned! The quest bringeth with it dire peril!" (Which is to say, "Be careful; it's dangerous.")

"A quest isn't supposed to be easy," the king said. He looked at his knights. "What do you say, my friends? Shall we go hunting?"

Before anyone could reply, one young man—

who wasn't even a knight yet—rose to his feet. He was named Givret, though few called him that. Nearly everyone referred to him as "that little fellow," because he was easily the shortest man at court. "My liege?" said Givret.

"Yes, Givret?"

"I wouldn't do this," said Givret.

Other knights stared at Givret, but the king only said, "Why not?"

"It docsn't seem wise, sire."

At that, Sir Lamorak the Hasty exclaimed, "Of course we should do it! *I'm* not afraid of dire peril."

"I agree!" shouted Sir Gareth the Valorous. "The direr the better, I say! If that little fellow is afraid, he doesn't have to come!"

Other knights joined in, calling for the hunt to begin and sneering at Givret's cowardice. Givret grew red, but he held his tongue.

At last another young man rose. This was Sir

Erec, a newly made knight and the son of King Lac of East Wales. Sir Erec cleared his throat. "My friends," he said. "You do wrong to call Givret a coward."

He smiled at Givret, then added, "After all, we shouldn't expect to find great hearts in little bodies." Givret didn't smile back.

King Arthur held up a hand. "Enough of this. Thank you for your advice, Givret, but I see no harm in this adventure. Let us go hunting!"

Within the hour all the court had gathered at the forest's edge for the hunt. Hounds bayed, horses snorted, and knights in bright hunting clothes milled about. Amid the splendor and confusion sat King Arthur's queen, Guinevere, on a white mare. When all the knights were ready to begin, King Arthur called out, "I need one man to stay with the queen, to be her guard and escort!"

There was a long silence. No knight wanted to be left behind. Then Givret urged his mount forward. "I will stay with Queen Guinevere, sire."

"Thank you, Givret," said the king. The hunting horn sounded, and a moment later Givret and the queen were alone.

"I thank you, too, Givret," said Queen Guinevere. "It must have been hard to volunteer to stay behind."

Givret shrugged. "Everyone thinks I'm a coward anyway."

"I do not," the queen replied. "But I cannot help wondering: Why *did* you advise against this hunt?"

Before Givret could reply, though, a strange knight in full armor rode out of the woods, followed by a lady on a gray mare. Givret wore no armor, but he had promised to protect Queen Guinevere, so he moved his own horse between

the knight and the queen. "Good day, Sir Knight," he said politely.

"Who are all these blundering fools riding through the forest, kicking up mud?" the strange knight demanded. "They nearly spattered my lady, the most beautiful lady in the world!"

"They meant no harm," Givret replied soothingly. "That was a hunting party from King Arthur's court."

"A hunting party that large? Ridiculous! My lady, who is the most beautiful lady in the world, scoffs at the very idea."

Givret glanced at the most beautiful

lady in the world. She was picking a bit of grit from under her thumbnail and paying no attention. "Er, if you say so, Sir Knight," Givret said.

"Why would so many go hunting at once?" the knight continued.

"You see, they're after a magical white stag," Givret explained.

"Magical? What do you mean?"

"It is said that whoever catches the stag earns the right to–" Givret broke off.

"Well? Right to do what?"

Givret shrugged. "The right to kiss the most beautiful lady in the world," he said.

"That they shall not!" roared the knight. "For *my* lady is the most beautiful lady in the world, and no one shall kiss her but I–Sir Yoder, son of Nut!"

"That's your name?" Givret asked. "Sir Yoder, son of . . . of . . ."

"Son of Nut, yes."

"I see. That would make me a bit testy, too," Givret commented.

Sir Yoder ignored him. "No other lady is so beautiful as my lady! Compared to her, even that lady beside you is a warty hag!"

Sir Yoder placed his hand on his sword, as if expecting Givret to react angrily, but Givret only replied, "If that is so, Sir Yoder, then you must capture the white stag yourself. You should join the hunt at once!"

Sir Yoder drew a sharp breath. "Why, you're right!"

"And I will help you," Givret continued. "For I happen to know that Arthur's knights are chasing the wrong stag! The *real* magical stag is in . . . in Scotland!"

Sir Yoder blinked. "Scotland? But that's days and days from here!"

"You'd better hurry, then," Givret said urgently,

"before someone else catches the stag and earns the right to kiss—"

"You're right again!" shouted Sir Yoder. "Come, my lady! To Scotland!" And off they rode.

Queen Guinevere began to giggle. "Thank you, Givret, for getting rid of our rude friend. But did you have to send him so far?"

"Nothing wrong with Scotland," Givret replied. "Besides, it serves him right; he insulted you."

Now a new voice broke in. "What was that? Someone insulted the queen?"

It was Sir Erec, the prince of East Wales, who was just emerging from the woods. "What are you doing back here, Erec?" asked the queen.

"I got separated from the others, then couldn't find my way back," Erec explained. "Odd thing, but trees all look alike. Ever noticed that? How anyone finds his way in a forest—but never mind that! Answer me! Did someone really insult the queen?"

"Yes," Queen Guinevere replied, "a wandering knight named Sir Yoder called me a warty hag."

"Sir Yoder, son of Nut," added Givret helpfully.

"And what did you do, Givret? Did you face him in single combat?"

Givret shook his head. "The thing is, Erec, this son of Nut chap was wearing armor, and I'm not. So I sent him to Scotland instead."

"You didn't fight him?" exclaimed Sir Erec in dismay.

"Only a fool would fight in hunting clothes," Givret said.

"I shall fight him myself!" Sir Erec declared. "To Scotland!" Spurring his horse, he bounded away.

"But Erec," called Queen Guinevere, "Sir Yoder has already been punished!" But Sir Erec was already gone. "Oh, dear," said the queen, shaking her head sadly.

CHAPTER 2
Sir Givret

As it turned out, King Arthur himself captured the white stag, but all the knights had a splendid day of hunting, and with great goodwill they returned to Camelot to celebrate their day with a feast. The goodwill lasted through the meal, and as the last dishes were being cleared, Arthur rose to his feet and said, "There is only one matter left to deal with. By capturing the stag, I have earned the right to kiss the most beautiful lady in the world." He turned toward Queen Guinevere.

"I suppose I have to allow it," interrupted one of Arthur's knights, Sir Gilbert the Lovestruck, with a sigh. "Here she is, Lady Mariana."

King Arthur hesitated. "Er, Lady Mariana?"

"Yes," declared Sir Gilbert, sighing again. "The most beautiful lady in the world!" Lady Mariana blushed, and King Arthur scratched his head. Things had gotten complicated.

Then another knight, Sir Cadmus the Handsome, rose. "Excuse me, Your Highness," he said. "I believe I can help you."

"Can you?" asked King Arthur. "I would be very grateful."

"Yes," Sir Cadmus said. "You should kiss *my* lady, Lady Gretchen."

Givret put his elbows on the table and covered his face with his hands.

Matters got worse. Sir Griflet the Tidy leaped to his feet. "I beg your pardon, Sir Cadmus, but *my* lady, Lady Winifred, is the most beautiful lady in the world!"

"Lady Winifred!" exclaimed Sir Cadmus with a snort. "Compared to my Gretchen? I'm afraid, my friend, that we'll have to change your name to Sir Griflet the Blind."

Sir Gilbert sniffed. "Well, if Sir Cadmus the Lackwit thinks that his Gretchen can hold a candle to my Mariana—"

All around the banquet hall, each lady began looking at her knight with raised eyebrows—as if to say, "Well?"—and the knights began to clear their throats and rise uncomfortably to their feet. "Actually, *my* lady is the most beautiful in the world!" . . . "No, *mine* is!" . . . "You're all off your heads! *My* lady is far more beautiful!"

Sir Cadmus turned to the king. "Sire!" he called

out. "I appeal to your judgment! Will you please tell Sir Griflet the Simplepate that compared to my Gretchen—"

"My liege," interrupted Sir Griflet, "if Sir Cadmus the Stable-Trash-for-Brains is quite finished, would you please declare that my Winifred is—"

"Silence!" commanded King Arthur. The room grew still. The king gazed sternly about the room, his eyes pausing briefly at Givret. "I will announce my decision in a moment," he said. "Ah, Givret, would you mind stepping aside with me for a moment?"

When the king and Givret were away from the others, King Arthur whispered, "Is this why you advised against the hunt?"

Givret nodded. "Yes, sire. You see, some knights will do anything to defend their lady's beauty."

The king grinned suddenly. "Some will even go to Scotland." Givret blinked with surprise, but the king said, "Guinevere told me how you got rid of that rude knight in the forest. Quite brilliant. I don't suppose you could fix up this mess so neatly, could you?"

Givret thought for a moment. "I can try," he said. He turned to the gathered knights. "My friends, the king has chosen the most beautiful lady in the world."

King Arthur looked alarmed, but his knights began calling out, "Who? Who is it?"

Givret waited until the room was quiet. "I think we *all* know which lady is the most beautiful," he said calmly. "After all, true beauty should be obvious to everyone, or what would be the point of it? And, since we all know who it is, I don't even need to say her name."

The knights glanced at each other uncertainly.

Givret continued, "Moreover, the king has decided that such a beautiful lady should only be

kissed by her own true love, so he freely surrenders his prize to that lady's knight."

Givret paused expectantly. The knights shuffled their feet and scratched their heads.

"Well?" Givret said. "Aren't you going to kiss her?"

With a start, all the knights realized that the tables had been turned on them. If each didn't kiss his own lady, and quickly, they would all have some explaining to do later. Every knight kissed his lady, and every lady smiled to know that her knight considered her the most beautiful lady in the world.

Then King Arthur, as soon as he had given Queen Guinevere a kiss, raised his hand and called out, "One moment! There is another matter to deal with! I have decided that not another hour shall pass before I grant knighthood to a deserving young man! Givret? Approach me at once and kneel!"

Several knights muttered, "What? That little fellow? What has *he* done to earn knighthood?"

Drawing his great sword Excalibur and laying it on Givret's shoulders, King Arthur said, "This day Givret has protected the queen from insult, and has done me a great service as well. These are deeds deserving of knighthood!"

The gathered knights muttered to each other, "Service? But who did he defeat in battle?"

King Arthur shook his head sadly. "Don't you fellows ever think of anything but fighting? There are many ways of serving your king." Turning back to Givret, he said, "I grant thee knighthood and fellowship at this table, and I dub thee Sir Givret the . . ." He paused. "The what? How shall you be known?"

"How about Sir Givret the Short?" called a voice.

King Arthur frowned. "I was about to suggest Sir Givret the Brilliant," he said.

Givret looked up. "Sire?" he said. "I'd rather be Sir Givret the Short."

The king stared at him. "You would?"

Sir Givret nodded. "It will be much easier to live up to. You see, I can't promise always to be brilliant."

King Arthur grinned. "Very well, then."

And so it was that Sir Givret the Short was made a Knight of the Round Table.

CHAPTER 3
Givret's First Quest

In those days it was the custom for a new knight to be sent out at once on a quest for adventures, so Givret was not at all surprised the next morning to be summoned to the king's presence.

"Maybe I'll be sent to fight a recreant knight," he mused. That was what people called the cowardly knights who bullied the weak. "Or maybe to slay a dragon."

"Sir Givret!" said King Arthur firmly when Givret arrived in the throne room. "I have chosen your first quest. I wish you to go to Scotland!"

"I beg your pardon, sire?" replied Givret.

"You are to seek out Sir Erec, prince of East Wales, your fellow Knight of the Round Table, help him complete his task, and bring him home safely."

"Help Sir Erec?" exclaimed Givret. "But—forgive me, my liege—Sir Erec is an idiot." King Arthur raised one eyebrow. "Honestly, sire! I mean, the fellow set out in hunting clothes to chase down a knight in armor, to make him apologize! Erec has goose down for brains!"

King Arthur finally spoke. "If that is so, then he needs your help more than ever."

"Look here," said Givret. "Haven't you got a dragon in need of slaying? Any recreant knights lurking about?"

"I have given you your quest," the king said.

"*Two* dragons?" Givret asked desperately, but King Arthur said nothing, and an hour later Givret was armored and on the Great North Road to Scotland.

The ride north was not very fun. The problem was Givret's size. Every time he passed through a town, people would laugh and call out things like, "Hey, boy! Does your father know you've pinched his armor?" and "I didn't know they knighted dwarfs!" Some knights might have had the laughing townspeople whipped—knights could do that sort of thing back then—but as a Knight of the Round Table Givret had promised to protect the weak, even the ones he didn't like, so he ignored the taunts and tried to avoid towns.

Givret did take action once, though. While skirting a village, he came upon a gang of boys throwing stones at an old man in a black cloak. Leaping from his horse, Givret took his riding whip to the seats of the boys' pants. A few yelps later, the boys were gone.

"Thank you, kind sir," wheezed the old man.

"You're welcome," replied Givret. "Why were those boys abusing you?"

"Oh, it's this cursed black cloak," the old man sighed. "I never should have bought it. It's soft and warm, but whenever people see a fellow in a black robe, they think he must be a sorcerer. They

either drive me away or run. Terrible for business, I can tell you."

"Business? What business?"

The old man smiled broadly. "I am Gaston the Peddler, bringing to England the latest fashions from Paris, France!"

"Are you indeed?" murmured Givret politely.

"Take this, for instance!" Gaston said, pulling a small dish from his cart. "It's all the rage, I assure you! It's called a finger bowl!"

"Very pretty. Um ... what does it do?"

"You fill it with water and then dip your fingers in it before eating!"

"Do you?" Givret said. "Why?"

"To wash them off, of course!"

"Wash *before* eating?" Givret asked, puzzled. "That makes no sense. I can see washing off all the grease and sauce *after* you've eaten, but why would you—?"

"Ah, but you won't *have* grease and sauce on your fingers after eating!" Gaston said eagerly. "Because of this other new invention! It's called ... a fork! You cut your meat into pieces with a knife, then pick up the bits with this!"

"Why?"

"So you don't get food on your fingers!"

Givret shook his head sadly. "Quite mad, you know. You want me to wash my hands before eating, then never touch my food anyway? No, thank you. But there is one thing I *would* like to buy."

"Yes?" said the peddler eagerly. "What is it?"

"Your black cloak."

Gaston agreed, and a few moments later Givret was pulling the cloak on over his armor. It covered it completely.

"Excellent!" said Givret. "If I were you, friend, I'd go into the clothing business and give up this rot about finger bowls and forks. You'll never make a living selling such nonsense."

"Ah, just wait," Gaston said. "The day will come when little boys all across England will wash their hands before meals and eat with forks."

Givret laughed. "Don't be silly. Boys will never buy such foolishness."

"No," the peddler said, smiling, "but their mothers will."

The next day Givret found Sir Erec. Rounding a bend in the Great North Road, he nearly ran right into the other knight, who was heading south.

"Erec!" Givret exclaimed.

"Why, Givret! How nice to see you!" Erec said, reining in his horse.

"I say, Erec, have you already caught up with that Sir Yoder fellow?" Givret asked hopefully. Erec shook his head, and Givret sighed. "Then where are you going?" he asked.

"To Scotland, of course," Erec said. "This is the Great North Road, isn't it?"

"Well, yes," Givret replied. "But you're going south on it."

Erec blinked. "Really? . . . I mean to say, well, I *did* get rather turned around in that last forest but . . . are you sure?" Givret nodded, and Erec said thoughtfully, "Then that explains it! The church in that last village looked *just* like one I'd passed earlier, but I decided it couldn't be the same, because it was on the other side of the road."

Givret stared at Erec for a moment, then said, "Right. Well, anyway, that way is definitely north. Shall we ride together?"

Erec agreed, and they set off, riding mostly in silence. Erec had little to say, and Givret was glad of it. Instead, he spent his time asking everyone they met if they had seen Sir Yoder. He had no luck, though, until they came upon a young herald. When asked about Sir Yoder, this herald replied, "An I could help thee I would most willingly, O fair and noble sirs, but I wit not of such a knight, nor have I heard of anyone y-clept 'Sir Yoder.' I crave thy pardon, your worships." (This meant, "Wish I could help, but I've never heard of him. Sorry.")

"No, no, don't mention it," Givret said. "But, say, I have another question."

"Ask whatsoever thou wilt, and be it in my power, I shall aid thee to the utmost!" ("Sure. Ask away.")

"I've been wondering this for ages: Do you heralds always talk like that? I mean, when you're at home with your family, do you spout off all that *thee* and *thou* and *y-clept* rot?"

The herald grinned and lowered his voice. "No, but don't tell anyone. It's part of the mystique of being a herald, using all those gold-plated words."

Givret chuckled. "Your secret is safe with me.

Well, if you ever deliver a message to Camelot, come look us up. I'm Sir Givret and this is Sir Erec. What's your name?"

The herald flushed slightly, then said, "Harold."

Givret's mouth dropped open. "Harold the Herald?"

Harold nodded glumly. "My father's idea. He's a herald, too, and he thought it was cute."

"I'm so sorry," Givret said sympathetically. "And when you have a son—?"

"Freddy," Harold said promptly. "I'll call him Freddy."

Givret nodded, then turned to Erec, who had been sitting in silence. "Well, Erec, we'd better go. We still have to find Sir Yoder and the most beautiful lady in the world."

"What did you say?" asked Harold suddenly. "About the most beautiful lady?"

"Oh, this Yoder chap we're looking for has a lady

with him. I don't know her name, but Yoder calls her 'the most beautiful lady in the world.' "

"Hmm," Harold murmured. "You might go to Limors and ask the count there, Count Oringle, if he's seen them."

"Why?" Givret asked.

"I've just come from Limors, where I was proclaiming a contest for the count, a test to choose the most beautiful lady in the land."

Remembering the quarrel that had nearly broken out at Camelot over the same question, Givret said, "Sounds daft. Why would the count want to hold such a contest?"

Harold shrugged. "I just proclaim; I don't ask questions. Maybe some fortuneteller told him to do it. Count Oringle's obsessed with spirits and such. He's always asking magicians and soothsayers for signs. I think he's a bit mad, but I'm careful not to say so in Limors."

"Why is that?"

Harold looked serious. "It's not a good idea to offend Count Oringle. He's a bad one. They say he's killed twelve men. But what I was thinking was that if this Yoder fellow's so proud of his lady, he might enter her in the count's contest."

Givret thanked Harold, and he and Erec set off for Limors.

CHAPTER 4
The Most Beautiful Lady in Limors

Givret and Erec arrived at Limors the next evening. They looked for a place to stay, but the only inn was full. The Beautiful Lady contest was to take place the next day, and all the rooms were taken by people who had come to watch.

"Why don't we ask this Count Oringle if he'll put us up?" Erec suggested. "After all, we're from the Round Table."

This wasn't a bad idea, really. In those days, it was common for traveling knights—especially those of Arthur's court—to stay with local nobles. Givret remembered what Harold the Herald had said about Count Oringle, but since he had no other ideas, he agreed. They made their way to a large, if rather shabby, house at the edge of the town, where Erec knocked.

An old man with a kind face opened the door. "Yes?"

"Is this the home of Count Oringle?" Erec asked.

The old man looked less kind. "No," he said shortly. "The count lives in the larger house on the other side of town."

He began to close the door, but Givret spoke. "Forgive us if we were rude, sir. We weren't looking for the count especially, but only for a place to stay the night. We are Sir Givret and Sir Erec of King Arthur's Round Table, and we've been on the road all day."

The old man relaxed and opened the door again. "Why didn't you say so? My home is yours." He showed them an empty stable for their horses, and a few minutes later they were walking together into a large, bare dining room.

"My name is Sir Valens," the old man said. "And I was just about to have my dinner. It's not much, but I would be honored to share it."

They accepted politely. Sir Valens didn't seem wealthy, but he treated his guests with an old-fashioned courtesy that put them at their ease.

When they were seated at the dining table, Givret asked Sir Valens if he had heard of a knight named Sir Yoder, son of Nut.

Sir Valens had not, and Erec added, "We thought he might come here because of this Beautiful Lady contest."

Sir Valens's face grew sad, and Givret asked quietly, "Could you explain this contest, sir? It seems an odd idea to me. Is Count Oringle a fool?"

In a low voice, Sir Valens replied, "No. The count is a villain, and he may be a madman, but he's no fool." He took a long breath, then said quietly, "Let me explain: This man Oringle came to Limors about ten years ago, at the head of an army of hired soldiers. He stole the castle of the former Count of Limors, and then proclaimed himself the new count."

Erec looked outraged. "Didn't the real Count of Limors fight back?" he demanded.

Sir Valens shook his head. "This was a peaceful

county, and the count was a peaceful man. He didn't even have any knights."

Erec's eyes blazed. "I would have *died* before I let someone steal my land and title!" he exclaimed.

Sir Valens smiled sadly. "But the old count had a young daughter. What would have happened to her if her father had been killed?"

While Erec thought about that, Givret asked, "What *did* become of the count and his daughter?"

"Oringle let them live in an old house nearby, where he could watch them, but he took their horses, so they became almost prisoners. Then, as the years passed, the old count's daughter grew into a beautiful woman, and Oringle decided to marry her. Of course, the old count refused to allow it."

Givret nodded. "Hmm. And did Oringle have the old count killed?"

"I see you've heard Oringle's reputation," said Sir

Valens. "No, the people of Limors still love the old count and might rise up against Oringle if he did that. Instead he came up with this Beautiful Lady contest. All the ladies in the land must go to the town square tomorrow to be judged, and the one who is chosen is required to marry the highest noble in Limors, which of course is Oringle. He'll choose the old count's daughter, then act as if he has no choice but to marry her, under the law."

Givret said, "But what if some other lady is more beautiful than the count's daughter?"

"Judge for yourselves," Sir Valens said. "I think I hear my daughter, Enide, coming now."

"*Your* daughter?" said Givret.

"Yes," said Sir Valens. "I am the old count."

Then the door opened and no one spoke for a long moment, because standing in the doorway was the most dazzlingly beautiful lady that either Givret or Erec had ever seen.

"My daughter, Lady Enide," said Sir Valens.

"Pleased to meet you, my lady," Givret said.

Erec said nothing. He only stared.

"Finding Sir Yoder will just have to wait," Givret said as soon as he and Erec were alone. "We must help Sir Valens and Lady Enide."

"Yes!" Erec agreed enthusiastically. "Enide must not marry that horrible count! I have an idea!"

"Er . . . you do?" Givret asked. This didn't sound like Erec, somehow.

"Yes! I shall take Enide away with me to East Wales, to the castle of my father, King Lac!"

"Riding double, I suppose?" asked Givret. "Remember, they have no horses."

Erec frowned. "But we *must* do something! Enide is perfection itself! Her face! Her eyes! And she's so clever, too!"

"*Clever?*" Givret repeated. Lady Enide was a beauty,

but at dinner it had occurred to Givret that he had never heard anyone say so much about so little for so long. "Don't worry, Erec," he said. "I have an idea, too. Now listen closely, because I need you to follow these instructions." He told Erec what to do the next day, made him repeat it several times, and then took his black cloak and slipped out into the night.

CHAPTER 5
Sir Erec's Brilliance

The contest for the most beautiful lady in Limors turned out as expected. Enide wore her plainest gown and left her hair uncombed and tangled, but nothing could disguise her beauty. "We have chosen a winner!" declared Count Oringle, a squat fellow with a bristly beard, once he had paraded all the ladies before the crowd. "And, since great beauty should be honored greatly, the winner gets to wed the greatest noble in Limors! Me!

The winner is . . . Lady Enide!"

All that morning, Givret had been standing concealed in a shadowy doorway, waiting for this moment. "You are mistaken, Count Oringle!" he shouted, stepping into the open. He wore his black robe with the hood pulled low over his face.

"Who the devil are you?" Count Oringle snapped.

"I . . ." Givret paused for effect. "I am a *sorcerer!* I bring a solemn message to Count Oringle from the Spirit World!"

A hush fell over the crowd, and Count Oringle turned pale. "A sorcerer!" he gasped.

"Yes!" Givret declared. "The dark spirits of Tara have sent you a message! Come here!"

"Of course, of course," the count said, bowing. "I'll just claim my new bride, and then—"

"Didn't you hear me?" Givret scoffed. "She is not your bride!"

"Don't you think she's the most beautiful lady?" Count Oringle asked.

"That's not the problem," snapped Givret. "*You* are not the greatest noble present!" Whirling on his heel, Givret pointed at Erec, who was standing beside Sir Valens. "*He* is! You! Knight! What is your name?"

Erec stepped forward and recited the words Givret had made him memorize. "My name is Sir Erec, of King Arthur's court, and my father is Lac, King of East Wales."

"A prince, as you know, is higher than a count," said Givret. "But enough of this! I have not come to settle silly contests but to bring you a word from the spirits."

Suddenly, Erec figured it out. "By Jove!" he exclaimed. "I *am* a prince! That means . . . by the rules, Enide is to marry . . ." Throwing himself forward, he knelt at Enide's feet, gazing up into her face, and said, "Will you marry me, dearest Enide? Please say yes!"

Trembling with fury, Count Oringle drew a long dagger from his belt and stepped toward Erec, but Givret had been watching for something like this. "Here is my message!" he shrieked. "The spirits of the men you have killed have cast a curse on you! If you should murder even *one* more man, that man's ghost will haunt you forever! Beware! The shades of the dead have spoken!"

Count Oringle dropped his dagger as if it were

red hot. Givret ducked out of sight—glad for once that he was so small—and stripped off his cloak. His plan had gone off without a hitch.

Then came a hitch. While Erec and Enide were still gazing into each other's eyes and the count still standing in frozen terror, a knight on horseback galloped into the square, scattering the crowd around him. "Who dares to crown the most beautiful lady in the land without consulting me?" called the knight. "*My* lady is the most beautiful in the land, and I—I, Sir Yoder, son of Nut—shall fight anyone who denies it!"

Of course, Erec leapt to his feet. "*I* deny it! Lady Enide is the most beautiful lady in the world!"

At once, both knights began hacking at each other with swords. Givret could only stare, helpless, while Erec, still dressed in his hunting clothes, fought with the fully armored Yoder—the very thing Givret had been sent to prevent.

But slowly, Givret's spirits began to rise. Somehow, even without armor, Erec was holding his own. In fact, he was fighting magnificently. *By George!* Givret thought. *Maybe Erec didn't need me after all!* It occurred to Givret that, while Erec might not win any prizes for his brains, there were other kinds of brilliance.

A moment later, with a splendid flick of his sword, Erec disarmed Sir Yoder, who sank, panting, to his knees at Erec's feet. "I yield!" he gasped. "Never have I seen such swordplay!"

"Then hear this, Sir Yoder, son of Nut," Erec said clearly. "I will spare your life, on two conditions. First, you must go to Camelot, to Queen Guinevere, and apologize for insulting her in the forest the day of the great hunt." Sir Yoder looked confused, and Erec said, "The lady that you called a warty hag was the queen. Second, you must promise to fight no more battles to defend your lady's beauty." Erec glanced at Enide, then added, "You know, if your lady loves you, that ought to be enough, don't you think?"

Sir Yoder bowed his head in acceptance, and the crowd roared its approval—they had had a *marvelous* day's entertainment. Then Erec turned back to Enide. "I'm sorry we were interrupted," he said, as soon as the cheering had subsided. "But you never had a chance to give me your answer. Will you marry me, Enide?"

"Yes, Sir Erec, I will!" Enide replied breathlessly.

And so it was that Sir Givret finished his first quest, and a fine quest it had turned out to be. Not only had Erec done what he set out to do, teaching Sir Yoder, son of Nut, a valuable lesson, but Lady Enide had been rescued from marrying the wicked Count Oringle, and she and Erec had found love. Even the crowd had had a grand time. Only Count Oringle had had a really bad day, and that didn't bother Givret at all.

CHAPTER 6

Sir Erec's Next Quest

Erec and Enide were married the next day. Givret rode back to Camelot to report on their adventures, while Erec bought two horses and took Lady Enide and her father to Wales, to present them to his father. King Lac was delighted with them both. He gave the happy couple their very own castle and made Sir Valens his chief advisor. It all felt like Happily Ever After.

But there's one thing about Happily Ever After

that storytellers sometimes forget to mention: It takes a while to get it right. You see, not everyone has the same idea of Happily Ever After. So, when two people try to find happiness together, there are always a few details to work out. Erec, for instance, thought happiness was either riding alone in search of adventures or sitting at home by a fire in peace and quiet. Enide, on the other hand, was happiest when she was talking. Well, it was a problem.

That was the situation that Givret found some six months later when he came for a visit. Erec received his friend with delight, and for several minutes they exchanged news. Then Givret asked, "So, how's married life?"

"It's wonderful!" Erec replied heartily.

"Good, good," Givret said, but after a moment, he asked, "Is it so wonderful that you've decided to give up adventures and knightly deeds for Enide?"

Erec stared at Givret. "What? Don't be silly! Why would you ask that?"

"That's what they're saying in the village," Givret said. "They're calling you, um, Sir Erec the Pussycat."

"I never said any such thing!" Erec exclaimed. "Enide's the one who visits the village, anyway."

At that moment, Enide burst into the room. "Givret!" she squealed. "They *told* me it was you, but I had to come see for myself! I'm *so* glad to see you! You look wonderful! Do you like my dress? Erec gave it to me yesterday, just as a present. He spoils me so! Are you well? But I can see you are! Did you just now arrive? Has Erec offered you anything to eat? We have some tea cakes with raspberries! Oh, dear, whoever would have thought that today we would get a visit from our very dearest friend? Without you we never would have met! Have you been riding all day? I like riding, too, but I haven't been out in, oh, forever, except for a few shopping trips to the village, just for things that we couldn't do without, and these darling buttons that I saw and just had to have. They'll be perfect on a pink dress, don't you think? If only I had one!"

Enide stopped to show Givret the buttons, and he managed to say, "I'm glad to see you, too, Enide," before she started again.

"I used to have a pink dress," Enide began, "but honestly, it had red ribbons on it, if you can imagine, and so I gave it away, but if I had—"

During all this, Erec had been gazing at Enide with suspicion dawning in his eyes. "Enide," he said. "Be quiet for a moment, can't you?"

Enide stared at Erec. He had never hushed her before.

"I have to ask you something," Erec said. "They're saying down in the village that I've promised to give up adventures forever for your sake. Do you know why people would think that?"

Enide clapped her hands to her mouth and giggled. "Oh, if that isn't the silliest thing! All I said was that you would rather be with me than go on adventures, like you said to me that night when you gave me those pearl earrings! It was *so* romantic! But I only told one person . . . no, wait, two—three! Plus the fishwife."

Erec turned red. "You told the whole village I was giving up being a knight for you? No wonder they're laughing at me!"

"Laughing at you! Oh, surely not!" Enide gasped.

"Givret?" said Erec.

Givret wished he hadn't brought the matter up, but he replied honestly: "Well, they are a bit. Maybe if Enide went back to the village and told people there that they have it wrong—"

"It's too late for that now," Erec declared angrily.

"I have to *prove* them wrong! Tomorrow morning I'm going questing!"

Enide looked stricken. "You're leaving me?" she whispered.

"I say, Erec," Givret began, "maybe you should think about this a day or two before—"

Enide burst into tears, drowning out the rest of his words. She cried and clutched her hair and said she was very sorry and would do anything to make it better, but she couldn't bear it if Erec went off and left her and so on. "I'll be lost without you!" she wailed.

"You should have thought of that before you went gossiping about me!" Erec snapped. Enide looked stunned.

"Well . . . can I go with you?" she asked softly.

Then Erec had an idea. Maybe it wasn't a great idea, but Erec hadn't had as much practice with ideas as Givret. "Yes, Enide," he said. "You can ride with me, but on one condition: as long as we travel, *you cannot speak a single word!*"

CHAPTER 7
The Silence of Lady Enide

When Givret woke the next morning, Erec's servants told him that their master had gone. He had left the castle hours before dawn, accompanied by a silent Lady Enide. Givret set out after them at once, following the servants' directions toward the northeast. Before long, he came upon three men in rough clothes huddled around a fire. Givret laid one hand on his sword—there were bandits in those forests—but these men were too busy with their own problems to be threatening. One man winced every time he moved his arm, another held his head in his hands, and the third rubbed a swollen knee. All three were very bruised and battered. Sore Arm saw Givret grasp his sword and said, "Don't waste yer time, sir. We won't hurt ye none."

"I thought you might be bandits," Givret explained.

The man rubbed his arm again, then said, "This morning ye'd have been right," he said. "But we're givin' it up. Unhealthy. That's what it is."

Head-in-Hands groaned and looked up. "'E took me club away and bonked me 'ead with it!" he said.

"Have you had some trouble?" Givret asked. "Trouble, he calls it!" snorted Sore Arm. "Ay, ye could say that."

"Me own club! And bonked me in the 'ead!"

Givret tried to look sympathetic. "I don't suppose you've met a wandering knight accompanied by a lady, have you?"

Sore Arm said, "Ay, that sounds like the fellow. Who *was* that?"

"That," Givret said carefully, "was the great Sir Erec of East Wales, gone out questing. You might tell that to people you meet."

"Why?" asked Sore Arm.

"Well, it's just that there's a rumor going about that Sir Erec has given up fighting."

"I wish that was so!" muttered Sore Arm.

"And the silent lady with him was his wife, Lady Enide," Givret added.

"Silent!" grunted Sore Arm. "I wish that was so, too."

"She wasn't silent?"

"Not when it mattered," Sore Arm said. "See, the

way we work—used to work, I mean—is two of us blocks the road while Clem there sneaks up behind a chap and lays him out with a club. It always works, but this time the lady sees Clem creeping up and shouts, 'Look out!' "

"What happened then?" Givret asked.

"'E TOOK ME CLUB AWAY AND BONKED ME OWN 'EAD WITH IT!" shouted Clem.

"Oh, right," Givret said. "You mentioned that, didn't you? Sorry."

"After that, he bonks the rest of us a bit," Sore Arm added. Then he frowned, looking very confused. "And when he's finished, the fellow starts yellin' at the lady for speaking, even though she's just saved his life. Tell me, is this Sir Erec barmy?"

Givret ignored the question. Tossing a few gold coins to the former bandits, he said, "Here. Live on this until you find honest work. You're making the right choice, you know. A bandit never knows when someone will take his club away and, um—"

"WE KNOW! WE KNOW!" shouted Clem.

Givret continued following Erec and Enide northeast, generally heading toward Limors. At dusk, Givret came upon four dusty and dented knights trudging down the path on foot. Now, knights *never* travel without horses—walking in armor is no fun—so Givret stopped and stared.

"What are you looking at?" growled a knight in

red armor. He carried a badly dented helmet under one arm, and one of his eyes was swollen nearly shut. With his other eye, he was gazing longingly at Givret's horse.

"It looks like a parade," Givret replied. "But your party costumes are all dented."

All the knights snarled at this, and Red said, "Why don't you get off that horse, little man, and say that?"

Givret stayed out of reach. He had never met a recreant knight, but he was pretty sure these knights were that sort. "No, thank you," he replied. "I may be little, but I'm not stupid. Not even Sir Lancelot would take on four knights at once."

At that, one of the knights said, "Say, maybe that's it! Maybe it was Sir Lancelot!"

"Shut up!" snapped Red.

"I mean, if we were beaten by Sir Lancelot, it wouldn't be so embarrass—"

"Shut your trap, I said!"

Givret laughed. "You don't mean it! All four of you were beaten by one knight? Alone?"

"He wasn't alone!" said Red. "He had someone with him!"

Then Givret understood. "No, he wasn't alone, was he? He had a lady with him."

"Well, the lady helped!" snarled Red. "If she had not called out a warning, we'd have taken him by surprise, and now we'd have ourselves two fine new horses!"

"Ah! So you meant to steal their horses, so after he'd beaten you, he took *your* horses, right? That's hilarious!" Givret laughed, but none of the knights joined him. After a moment Givret asked, "Say, did the knight seem annoyed at the lady for warning him?"

At this, all the knights turned toward Givret, and Red muttered, "Ay, that he did. He got angry with her for saving him, which made no sense at all. How did you know that? Do you know this knight?"

"I do," replied Givret.

The knight who had spoken before asked eagerly, "Is it Sir Lancelot?"

"No," said Givret. "It was Sir Erec of East Wales."

"What?" gasped Red. "The very one they say has given up fighting so as to hang about his lady's skirts?"

"That's what the rumor says," Givret agreed. "But it isn't true."

"No bleeding joke!" grumbled Red, and Givret rode on.

Givret hadn't caught up with Erec and Enide by nightfall, so he made camp and went to sleep. Before long, though, he was awakened by approaching footsteps. He grabbed his sword, but it was not an attacker who stumbled up to his campfire.

"Enide!" Givret cried.

"Oh, Givret! It's you!" Enide gasped with relief. Then she burst into tears.

Givret let her cry herself out, which took several minutes, then asked, "What are you doing out here alone?"

"Oh, it was just too awful!" Enide wailed. "I tried not to talk, really I did, as hard as I could, because I love Erec so much, but when those people attacked him, I *had* to warn him, didn't I? But then he was so angry and I saw that I could never be a good wife. I might as well be miserable with Count Oringle, if it will make dear Erec happy, but oh, I don't *want* to!"

"Hang on there, Enide," Givret asked. "Who said anything about Count Oringle?"

"Oh, we ran into him just as we were making

camp this evening—did you know we were back in Limors? Erec had no idea we'd gone this direction!—and the count seemed very friendly, but when Erec went to see to our horses, he whispered to me that he has a hundred soldiers just over that hill, and if I don't leave Erec and go to him before morning, he'll send them to kill Erec! So I decided that since I can't make Erec happy anyway, I can at least save his life, so I'm going to leave with horrid Count Oringle, and if I'm very, very lucky, maybe I'll die young."

Givret considered this. "Let me think a moment . . . No, there has to be another way. Tell you what, Enide: you go back to Erec, and I'll go see if the wicked count really has any soldiers over that hill."

"You think he might have been lying? I didn't think of that!"

Givret smiled reassuringly. "It's possible. I'll just

make sure. The important thing is for you to go back to Erec. I'll see you in the morning."

"But what will you do?"

Givret smiled again, with more confidence than he felt. "Trust me. I'll think of something."

A few minutes later, Givret was on the top of a nearby hill, looking down on a military camp large enough for at least a hundred men. "Bother," he said. "Oringle *wasn't* lying."

CHAPTER 8

The Battle of the Hundred Knights

Even in the middle of the night, Count Oringle's camp was busy as the army prepared for battle, so it was easy for Givret to stroll into the camp and take a seat by a fire without being noticed. He still didn't have a plan, but he thought something might come to him.

After a moment, a soldier sat beside him, and

together they watched two other soldiers sharpening their swords. "Silly duffers," the first soldier said, pointing at the sword sharpeners. "What do they need sharp swords for, if we ain't allowed to kill this Sir Erec?"

"We're not to kill Sir Erec?" Givret asked, surprised.

"Hadn't you heard?" the soldier asked. "The count's dreadful afraid of some prophecy or other, so he doesn't kill people anymore, just tosses them into his dungeons. We have to take Sir Erec alive, and since it's a hundred to one, we'll have him locked up before breakfast."

So Oringle still believed the prophecy Givret had invented! A plan began to form in Givret's mind. "If we live that long," he said mournfully. "If only I'd known it was Sir Erec we were against! I'd never have joined up."

"Eh?" the soldier asked.

"Haven't you heard about Sir Erec?" Givret asked.

"Heard what?"

Givret shook his head. "Never mind. I'm not supposed to say."

"Say what?" the soldier demanded.

Givret allowed the soldier to ask twice more, then leaned close and said, "Well, all right, but you have to promise not to tell a soul, you hear? This is in *strictest* confidence!"

"On my honor!" promised the soldier.

Givret lowered his voice. "This Sir Erec is no ordinary knight. An enchanter protects him with black magic. No weapon can touch him, and he's got a magic sword that cuts through armor like warm butter. How are we supposed to take a fellow like that alive?"

The soldier's mouth dropped open. "I don't believe all that," he said at last.

"Ask anyone," Givret said. "Sir Erec's the one who fought Sir Yoder at that Beautiful Lady contest the count held last year. Maybe you were there?"

The soldier caught his breath and nodded. "*That* was Sir Erec?" Then his eyes widened. "And there *was* an enchanter there!"

"Mum's the word, though," Givret cautioned. "We don't want to discourage the others."

The soldier nodded, but a few moments later he stood up and sauntered away. Soon he was whispering to another soldier. Givret smiled and lay down for a few hours' sleep.

By the time Count Oringle mustered his troops at dawn, his hundred knights had mysteriously become seventy-five. A quarter of his army had slipped off during the night, and from their expressions, the rest were wishing that they had thought of it. The count went into a rage, cursing the departed knights, but there was nothing he could do but tell the others to mount up and follow him. In the hubbub of saddling up and forming lines, five more knights disappeared.

Givret rode along. He planned to work his way to the back and, once the battle began, attack the army from the rear, but no matter how much he slowed down, none of the soldiers behind would pass. Finally, the one just to his rear said, "You're wasting your time. We *all* want to be at the back. Not that it'll matter, from what I hear."

"What *do* you hear?" Givret asked.

"They say this Sir Erec is like a demon, eight feet tall with tusks like a boar's. He sometimes kills ten or fifteen knights before breakfast just to work up an appetite."

"Is *that* what they say?" Givret asked, impressed.

"I figure we'll all die," the knight muttered, "if we're lucky. Better to die than to be turned into a beetle."

"Better than . . . er . . . I'm sorry, but you've lost me."

"That's what that black-robed enchanter of Erec's does. Turns people into dung beetles. I hope I die fighting."

"Maybe it wouldn't be so bad, being a dung beetle," Givret mused. "Once you got used to the smell, of course." He allowed this to sink in, then added, "All the same, I'd rather be a living knight. Maybe once the fighting starts, a fellow could slip off."

Then the army rode over a hill, and there was Erec, armed and armored and calmly facing his enemies alone.

"There he is!" shouted Count Oringle. "Now remember, take him alive! Charge!"

But the one who charged was Erec. The count's soldiers stared at him for a second, then scattered. In the confusion, Givret calmly drew his black cloak from his gear and pulled it on. Lifting his

arms, he called out, "I am Givret the Marvelous, Enchanter of Tara!" The handful of soldiers who remained stared at him, frozen with terror, and Givret added, "BOOGA-BOOGA-BOOGA!"

That did it. The last knights screamed and fled, leaving Count Oringle alone. The count looked to his right, then to his left, then gave his horse the spurs and disappeared in a cloud of dust. Only Givret and Erec were left of the Battle of a Hundred Knights.

"Givret?" Erec said. "What are you doing here?"

"Oh, I was just passing through, heard about this battle, and came along to lend you a hand."

"That was thoughtful of you," Erec said. "Who knows—if they hadn't been such cowards, I might have needed some help."

Then Enide stepped from behind a tree, where she had been hidden. She smiled at Givret, but her smile faded when Erec turned to look at her. "As for you, my lady," he said sternly, "this is now the third time you have disobeyed and spoken to me!"

"Did you warn him?" Givret asked Enide.

She nodded. "When you didn't come to our camp this morning, I decided I had to," she explained. "And I'm glad I did."

"There you go again!" said Erec. "If you loved me, you would be silent!"

"Erec," Givret said, "I like you, and you must be the bravest knight who ever lived, but sometimes you're also a prize looby. If Enide hadn't warned you, you'd be dead at least twice by now. Are you saying that if she really loved you she'd have let you die?"

"Never mind, Givret," Enide said miserably. "I'm tired of it, and I can't do it anymore. Maybe I do talk too much—well, all right, I know I do. I'll try to do better, but I won't try to be someone I'm not. Givret, would you take me home?"

"Home? You mean you're leaving?" asked Erec. He looked suddenly forlorn.

Givret looked for a moment at the two unhappy lovers, then said, "Look, I don't pretend to know much about romance, but I do know this, Erec. You're going to have to choose whether you want silence or Enide, because you can't have both at once."

Erec took a deep breath and let it out in a sigh. "Then I choose Enide."

"And I choose you, Erec," Enide said. "I love you."

Erec leapt from his horse and the two lovers flung themselves into each other's arms. Givret turned his mount. "As for me," he said, "I choose to leave you two alone. You'll have a lot to talk about."

CHAPTER 9

Givret the Marvelous

All seemed well again between Erec and Enide, and so long as he was in the neighborhood, Givret decided to drop in on his friend Harold the Herald. As it turned out, this was a lucky thing, because heralds always get all the latest news first. On Givret's third day there, Harold said, "Say, do you remember that count I told you about once—Oringle?"

Givret looked up quickly. Out of respect for Erec

and Enide's privacy, he hadn't told Harold about his recent dealings with the count. "I remember. What about him?"

"I just heard he's getting married next week. I feel sorry for the poor lady."

"I do, too," Givret said with feeling.

"Oh, well," Harold said. "Maybe this Lady Enide knows what she's getting into."

Givret left for Limors at once, asking everyone he met for news of Lady Enide or Sir Erec. The fourth person he met, a priest, confirmed Givret's worst fears.

"Ah, Sir Erec," the priest sighed. "Dead!"

Givret swallowed, his heart heavy. "How did he die?" he asked.

"Bravely!" the priest said. "He was rescuing a knight from two giants who had taken him captive. He killed both of the giants, too!"

"Did you see it happen?" Erec asked.

"No," replied the priest. "A villager who was there told me. I went to see if I was needed to perform last rites, but by the time I got to Count Oringle's castle, the poor knight was already dead."

"Hold on there," interrupted Givret. "Did you say Count Oringle's castle?"

"Yes. They say the count took pity on poor Lady Enide and brought her and Sir Erec's body to his castle."

Givret blinked. "The count took *pity?*" he repeated. "Count *Oringle?*"

The priest shrugged. "There's a first time for everything, my son."

Givret didn't believe it. Putting on his black sorcerer's robe, he went to the count's castle and demanded entry, only to be told that no one was allowed in without the count's approval. Givret turned away, thinking furiously. He had to find out what was up. And if, as he suspected, Lady Enide was the count's prisoner, he had to rescue her.

Then, walking through the village of Limors, Givret heard a familiar voice. "No, no, my lady, like this: Dip your fingers in the finger bowl and swirl them about . . . No, *before* you eat. Oh, yes, I promise you, that's how the fine ladies of Paris do it!"

Givret smiled suddenly. "Gaston!" he cried.

"Why, my lord Sir Givret!" exclaimed Gaston the Peddler, immediately leaving the lady he had been talking to. "How wonderful to see you! And in your black robe, too!"

"You wouldn't believe how useful it's been," Givret said. "Listen, Gaston, do you ever sell your wares at weddings?"

Gaston's eyes lit up. "All my best sales are for weddings! Brides will buy *anything,* the more useless the better! Do you know of a wedding nearby?"

"Do I ever! Count Oringle himself is getting married!"

"The count!" Gaston repeated, rubbing his hands gleefully. "I have just the thing! Salad forks!"

"I beg your pardon?"

"I told you about forks, didn't I? I thought I had. Well, this is even fruitier! A *second* set of forks to use for salad, and here's the best bit: *They're exactly the same!*"

"You're joking," Givret said, in awe.

"No, really! Everyone thinks they're different, so they buy a second set of forks and scatter them about their tables willy-nilly! I'll soon be able to retire, just on my profits from salad forks alone!"

Givret shook his head and asked, "What's a salad?"

Gaston giggled. "Raw vegetables, mostly. It

doesn't matter, so long as they have a special fork for it."

"You're either a madman or a genius," Givret said, "but I've no time to figure it out now. Listen, Gaston, could you get me into the count's castle unseen?"

"Nothing easier," Gaston said. He opened a door in his peddler's cart, revealing a shelf stuffed with trinkets and silks and ribbons. "Climb in here."

Givret was glad he was so small; a larger man would never have fit into Gaston's tiny cart. Even Givret barely managed to squeeze in, but soon Gaston was wheeling him toward Oringle's castle.

"Open up, my good man," Gaston cried to the guards. "I am Gaston, of Gaston's Exclusive Parisian Boutique, come all the way from France for the count's wedding." At first the guards repeated what they had told Givret, that no one was allowed in, but Gaston said, "Very well. *You* ex-

88

plain to your master why you sent away the finest wedding goods anywhere," and a moment later they were inside.

While the guards hurried to fetch the count, Gaston let Givret out. Tugging his black hood low over his face, Givret slipped into the shadows. "Keep the count busy as long as you can," he said, and then he hurried off. First he had to find Enide; only then could he make plans for getting her away. For the next half-hour, he ran down castle halls, tried doors, and peered around corners, but Enide was nowhere to be found.

Givret found something else, though. In a torch-lit room at the end of a long hall was Erec's body, laid out on a stone slab in full armor except for his helmet, which was the custom for slain knights. Givret knew he should hurry to find Enide, but he couldn't just pass by. Standing beside the body, he

reached out to stroke his friend's cheek. "Farewell,
old friend," he said, "I wish I... I... I *say!*"

Erec's skin was warm.

Givret's mouth dropped open. "For heaven's
sakes, Enide," he muttered, "didn't you even check
to see if he was dead? Erec! Get up!" He gave Erec
a shake.

Erec's eyelids flickered, and he frowned slightly. "Ouch," he murmured. "Head hurts. Go 'way. Want go back sleep."

Givret stopped shaking. "Yes, go back to sleep," he said. "That's a much better idea. I'll come get you when it's safe."

Now Givret searched even harder, and at last he was rewarded. Behind the last door in the longest corridor, he heard a woman crying. Givret burst into the room, and there was Enide, alone, sobbing into a pillow.

"Enide!" he cried. "Get up! Erec is—"

"Oh, Givret!" wailed Enide. "It's so sad! What shall I do without Erec?"

"Listen to me, Enide—"

But Enide didn't listen. "It was so horrible!" she sobbed. "He went off to fight those two giants and told me to stay behind and I didn't know what to do but I could hear him fighting and the giants were roaring and I was so scared and then Erec didn't come back and I didn't know what was happening!"

"Enide! I have to tell you—"

"So I went to see and when I got there the two giants were dead and the knight that Erec had saved was saying he had died bravely and so did the villagers there, and I cried and cried!"

"But you didn't actually check Erec, did you?" Givret said.

"And that's when Count Oringle came and he was much nicer than he'd ever been before and he said that Erec was a hero—which is true!—and I know I ought to be grateful to him for taking me in while he prepares the funeral, even if he *is* a rotter."

"Did he mention that he's also preparing a wedding?" asked Givret.

Enide stared. "No. Who's getting married?"

"You and the count," Givret said.

Enide's mouth dropped open. "What?" Then she demanded, "Is *that* what he's after?"

"Isn't it what he's always been after?" Givret asked.

"What a stinker!" Enide exclaimed indignantly. Just then footsteps came clicking down the corridor, and Givret barely had time to step into the shadows and pull his cloak around him before the door opened and Count Oringle himself entered.

"My lady," the count began, "I've come to see how—oh, good! You've stopped crying! I was starting to worry. Sir Erec was a great knight and all that, but two days without stopping *does* seem like it ought to be enough. Anyway, I've got something to show you."

Enide glared at the count, but he paid no attention. Producing two forks, he said, "My lady, if someday you should ever again feel like eating at a banquet, a wedding banquet, for instance, would you need *two* forks or just one?"

"What's a fork?" asked Enide.

"The latest thing from Paris," the count explained.

Enide drew herself up with dignity. "My husband isn't even buried yet! Why are you babbling to me about forks?"

Givret saw his opportunity. Stepping from the shadows as if materializing from the air, he announced loudly, "I'll tell you why he speaks of forks! Because he plans your wedding!"

"You again!" Count Oringle gasped.

"Yes! It is I! Givret the Marvelous, Enchanter of Tara!"

The count turned pale. "How did you get in here?"

Givret laughed. "Did you think mere gates and guards could keep me out? I go where I wish to go. I see what I wish to see. I know your private thoughts and wedding plans! But what woman will marry a man who will be haunted for eternity?"

Count Oringle took a step backward. "No!" he said. "I've kept your word! I've killed no one since the prophecy!"

"You are mistaken, O count," Givret said solemnly. *"You have slain Sir Erec the Brave!"*

"Did not!" protested the count. "He was killed by a giant! He hit him on the head!"

"That's true, you know," said Enide. "I thought I told you—"

Givret interrupted quickly. "The giant only wounded Sir Erec!" he declared. "He was still alive when he was brought to this castle! If you had cared for him, he would be alive to this day!" That much, at least, was true. "But because you did nothing, his death is *your* fault. The blame is *yours!*

Sir Erec's ghost will follow you from this day forth!"

The count began to tremble. "Isn't there anything I can do?"

Givret paused dramatically. "There is but one hope for you! If you give up your lands, leave England forever, and go to Rome to make confession to the pope, then you may be spared from the spirit's vengeance!"

"Give up my lands?" repeated Count Oringle, horrified.

"It's your choice," Givret said. "Either leave England now or spend the rest of your life with a ghost who thirsts for revenge."

The count hesitated, his fear at war with his greed. "Thirsts for revenge?" he repeated.

So intent were they all that none of them had noticed footsteps approaching, but just then the chamber door swung open and there on the threshold stood Erec himself. He was pale and unsteady, but he was standing without help. "Excuse me," he said, "but I'm thirsty."

Enide let out a piercing scream and swooned. Count Oringle, his eyes bulging and his face whiter than Erec's, made a noise like someone squeezing a frog, rushed from the room, and threw himself from the nearest window. Erec rubbed his temple, looked about for a moment, then said mildly, "What's wrong with them? All I wanted was a drink of water."

After that, matters sorted themselves out nicely. Count Oringle survived his leap from the window by landing in a manure cart, after which he caught a horse and started toward Rome, to make his confession to the pope. There he became a priest and changed his name to Innocent—it was never clear who he was trying to fool by that—

and he never went back to England. His castle, lands, and title were restored to Sir Valens, who ruled Limors wisely and well.

Erec and Enide returned to Wales, where they were much beloved for their fairness and compassion, if not always for their wisdom. But even if they weren't the brightest rulers ever, they were at least smart enough to listen to advice (something that many so-called clever people are too silly to do), and so they did very well indeed. They loved each other more every day, even when they disagreed about such things as which fork to use with the salad, and so they found their Happily Ever After at last. Gaston the Peddler became a regular visitor at their home, and Enide became quite his favorite customer, always willing to try the latest useless fashion, even ridiculous things like napkins, embroidered handkerchiefs, and soap.

As for Givret, he divided his time between

Camelot and Wales, but wherever he went he was treated with respect and his advice was sought out by all and treasured when received. Most people still called him Sir Givret the Short (although no one would dream of calling him "that little fellow" now), but King Arthur usually referred to him as Sir Givret the Wise. Even that was not enough for Erec and Enide—or, in years to come, to their many children. To them, he would always be Givret the Marvelous.